Steve was all packed.
He gave his dog, Fudge,
a hug.

Then Steve gave his
mom and his dad hugs.

Steve was going to
Hedgehog Lodge for the
weekend with his friend
Greg and Greg's dad,
Mr. Bridges.

In his backpack, Steve had wedged his pillow, a pair of shorts, a sports badge, and a picture of Fudge.

Steve showed Greg his sports badge. "This is for soccer," he said.

They left the city. They drove and drove until they crossed a bridge. It led down to a big lake.

Then they drove on a road at the edge of the lake. At last Mr. Bridges said, "We are nearly there. The lodge is just past that last ledge."

When they reached Hedgehog Lodge, Steve got out of the car. He felt so small next to all the tall trees.

When they went inside
the lodge, Steve and
Greg saw fishing poles
on the walls. Greg saw
a big fish.

"Let's race to the lake,"
said Greg.

Mr. Bridges watched as
Steve and Greg dove and
swam in the lake.

When they swam back,
Mr. Bridges said, "It
is time to go up to the
lodge for dinner, but
we can come back for
a campfire."

They had hot dogs and
beans for dinner back
at the lodge. They
made some friends, too.

After dinner, they went
back down to the lake.
As the sun set, the sky
turned red, yellow,
and pink.

At the campfire, they roasted marshmallows and did storytelling.

Steve could not wait
to tell Fudge all about
Hedgehog Lodge!